First published in 1988
3 5 7 9 10 8 6 4 2
© Text John Bush © Illustrations Paul Geraghty 1988
John Bush and Paul Geraghty have asserted their right under
the Copyright, Designs and Patents Act, 1988,
to be identified as the author and illustrator of this work

First published in the United Kingdom in 1988 by
Hutchinson Children's Books
Random House UK Limited
20 Vauxhall Bridge Road, London SW1V 2SA

Random House Australia (Pty) Limited
20 Alfred Street, Milsons Point, Sydney,
New South Wales 2061, Australia

Random House New Zealand Limited
18 Poland Road, Glenfield
Auckland 10, New Zealand

Random House South Africa (Pty) Limited
PO Box 337, Bergvlei, South Africa

Random House UK Limited Reg. No. 954009

A CIP catalogue record for this book
is available from the British Library

ISBN 0 09 173592 0

Printed in China

The
cross-with-us rhinoceros

John Bush and Paul Geraghty

Hutchinson

London   Sydney   Auckland   Johannesburg

To Pat and Garth

There was Willy, there was Wally, there was Tilly, there was I;
Four fine brave adventurers, beneath a bright blue sky.

We were full of fun and laughter until Tilly turned and said,
'What's that Willy? Look there Wally! What's that up ahead?'

We looked. We blinked. We looked again. We blinked. It was still there –

A huge great, grey rhinoceros, sniffing at the air.

He cocked his ears. He dropped his head. A huge foot pawed the ground.
And then that rhino turned on us and started charging down.

'I think that great rhinoceros is very, very cross with us;
VERY VERY cross with us,' said I.
'He must be very cross with us, he's charging down on top of us.
A cross-with-us rhinoceros! But why?'

'Gosh!' said Willy. 'Oooh!' said Wally.
Tilly stammered, 'G-g-golly! G-g-goodness! M-m-me oh my!'
'Come on,' I called, 'no time for that. Let's run before we're all squashed flat.'
Willy wailed, 'I wish that we could fly.'

With the rhino behind Willy,

And Willy behind Tilly, and Tilly behind Wally behind me;
We hurtled headlong through the grass, that rhino gaining on us fast,

Until we found a safe and sturdy tree.

Up we scrambled, up we hurried,
Up and up and up we scurried.
Up we fled for all that we were worth,

While that cross-with-us rhinoceros
Sniffed and snuffed and snorted,
As he stomped his rough, round feet into the earth.

Willy wept. Wally moaned.
'How long will we be here?' he groaned.

Poor Tilly was so scared she couldn't speak.
Then, looking down, I noticed

That the cross-with-us rhinoceros
Had lain down in the sun and gone to sleep.

Down we crept, while he slept.
We thought that we'd escape,
But as we tiptoed quickly off

We heard that rhino wake.

The thunder started up again, the thunder of those feet,
And closer, ever closer, came that dreadful, drumming beat.
We scuttled up a nearby hill

And down the other side.

There we saw a sight which made us all go weak inside.
A river deep. A river wide. I cried, 'We just can't win!'
'Why?' you ask. I'll tell you why: none of us could swim.

We closed our eyes.
Was this the end?
We had nowhere to go.

But then we heard that rhino stop,
Yes, STOP, and say, 'Hello.'

That cross-with-us rhinoceros, he stopped and said, 'Hello.'
A cross-with-us rhinoceros would never behave so.
Clearly that rhinoceros was never, ever cross with us.

'I followed you,' he said, 'to be your friend.'
'Why, how nice,' we cried as one. He took us riding in the sun.
And so our story had a happy end.